NOV   1994

11/28/94			
6/17/14			
(24)			
No owner			

HERE COMES HENNY

By Charlotte Pomerantz
Pictures by
Nancy Winslow Parker

Greenwillow Books, New York

Watercolor paints, colored pencils, and a black pen
were used for the full-color art. The text type is Cheltenham ITC.
Text copyright ©1994 by Charlotte Pomerantz
Illustrations copyright © 1994 by Nancy Winslow Parker

Printed in Hong Kong by South China Printing Company (1988) Ltd.
First Edition 10 9 8 7 6 5 4 3 2 1

Library of Congress Cataloging-in-Publication Data
Pomerantz, Charlotte.
Here comes Henny / by Charlotte Pomerantz ;
pictures by Nancy Winslow Parker.
p.   cm.
Summary: Henny carries to her picky chickies a sacky
in which she has pack pack packed snicky-snackies.
ISBN 0-688-12355-4 (trade).   ISBN 0-688-12356-2 (lib. bdg.)
[1. Chickens—Fiction.   2. Stories in rhyme.]
I. Parker, Nancy Winslow, ill.   II. Title.
Pz8.3.P564He   1994   [E]—dc20
93-5480   CIP   AC

For Margaret M. Burns
and her chicky-chicks, Madeline and Valerie
—C. P.

For the ladies on the porch
—N. W. P.

CLUCK!

Here comes Henny
with her sacky,

which she carries
pickabacky

back and forth
and forth and backy.

See her pick pick pick
a snicky.

See her pack pack pack
a snacky.

See her put
a snicky-snacky

in her backpack
picnic sacky.

CLUCK!

"Mommy, dearest,"
  said a chicky,
"did you pack pack pack
  a snacky?

Did you pick pick pick
  a snicky?

Did you put
  a snacky-snicky

in your backpack
picnic sacky?"

"No.

"I pick pick picked
 a snicky

and I pack pack packed
a snacky

and I put a
snicky-snacky

in my backpack
picnic sacky,

which I carried
pickabacky

back and forth
and forth and backy."

CLUCK!

"We won't eat
a snicky-snacky.

We eat only
snacky-snicky.

WE DEMAND A
SNACKY-SNICKY

for the chickies'
picnic-nicky."

So. . .
Henny took took took
a snicky,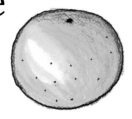

and she took took took
a snacky,

and she ate the
snicky-snacky,

THE ENTIRE
SNICKY-SNACKY.

When there was no more
snicky-snacky,

she laid her head
upon her sacky. . . .

All she heard was
"peep peep peep"

as she gently
fell asleep.

"Cheep cheep,"
said a hungry chicky.

"Maybe we have been
too picky."

So they slid away
the sacky,

which they all dragged
forth and backy.

And they pack pack packed
a snacky,

and they pick pick picked
a snicky,

and they crammed in
snacky-snicky

till it burst
with snacky-snicky

for the chickies'
picnic-nicky.